Dragon Found

By:

Ashley Brittany Kough

Legal Dragon Found

All rights reserved. No part of this book may be used or reproduced in any manner whatsoever without written permission of the writer, except in the case of brief quotations.

Copyright © 2018 Ashley Brittany Kough
All characters, places and events in this book are fictitious. Any resemblance to real places, events, or persons, living and dead is purely coincidental.
Published April 2018 by Ashley Kough

ISBN: 9781731496911

Cover Art ©Deanna Cathcart

This book is dedicated to Our Heavenly Father whom all inspiration comes from and to everyone who chases after the truth bravely.

− 1 −

Peering out the round loft window, Ashwyn stood dressed in her dark green leggings, tunic and brown boots, looking out into the darkness. The stars were slowly starting to fade as the sun crept slowly over the horizon. The dragons would be flying back to the caverns soon and she didn't want to miss watching them come in. This was her favorite time of day. Grabbing two apples off the table in the kitchen, she crept out her cottage and ran through the meadow to the top of the grassy hill where she knew Eli would be waiting for her.

"I hear their wings, you should be able to see them any moment" Eli smiled in her direction, his eyes never focusing on her.

Eli was not only Ashwyn's very best friend, he was also blind. Eli wasn't always blind though and he could remember many things, but most of all he liked remembering the dragons. He made up for his lack of eyesight with his acute hearing.

"I see them!" Ashwyn sat down next to him excitedly, handing him one of the apples, biting into the crunchy fruit, wiping the juice from her chin with the sleeve from her tunic. "Oh! They are gorgeous. The young ones are coming in first, chasing each other through the air. There's Rosalyn!"

An old dragon with impressive pink scales and black horns that rounded back against her head and along her neck. This was the dragons Queen. Ashwyn and Eli had never met her in person, but Gladiair assured them she looked fierce, but she was good and just.

She roared as she flew past them on her way to her cavern home in the mountain side under which they sat. Ashwyn jumped up as the dragons came in, spreading her arms out and running along the grass underneath them. Watching their scales of orange, pink, purple and green glisten like jewels, wishing she was one of their riders. Gladiair spotted her racing along, and took a quick dive towards her with, claws outstretched.

Almost got you.

His voice boomed in her mind as she was swiftly lifted off the ground squealing in delight. He glided low to the ground, so her boots kicked up wildflowers splashing them onto Eli. Gladiair hovered steadily lowering Ashwyn slowly back down to the ground, before he landed next to Eli.

Beautiful day for a flight. Now who wants to come and watch the Chosen? He said cheekily.

Ashwyn and Eli couldn't believe what they had just heard. Gladiair knew better than anyone, the choosing of the dragons and riders was a sacred event. Usually only the village elders, the humans that were to be chosen, and dragons could watch the ceremony. However, dragons were highly respected and talked to few humans, so being invited by one was rare. Eli quickly stood on his wood staff and made his way up to Gladiar.

It amazes me the speed you have with no eyesight little human.

He always addressed them as *little humans.* Gladiair was a beautiful yellow dragon. He was still considered young amongst his kind, a bit reckless and overly adventurous some would say. He had taken to Ashwyn and Eli when they were young, and he had found them adventuring in the nearby forest and enjoyed their company. Dragons weren't supposed to allow anyone to ride on them, other than their chosen rider. However, since Gladiair hadn't been officially chosen yet, he allowed Ashwyn and Eli to ride on him. He had hoped to be chosen today at the ceremony. All male dragons were considered for the honor of carrying a rider, but not all were chosen. Many factors went into the process. Some dragons were far to temperamental, and preferred a solitary life opposed to a constant connection with a human. Others were carriers of wisdom and truth, so chose more diplomatic roles. Gladiair was hoping to be bonded with a warrior and join the ranks to defend against evil. A young dragon wasn't supposed to leave the meadow without the permission of the Queen or Dragon Council. However, some had grown tired of waiting to be chosen and wanted their freedom, so had decided to leave on their own. They were however considered to be rouges and lived their life outside of dragon rule and protection.

"Gladiair?" Eli asked as the two scrambled up his scales onto his back. "How does the Dragon Council choose which dragons will be bonded?"

"They take any dragon into consideration who volunteers. Queen Rosalyn assigns the rest" he said.

Gladiair had volunteered to fulfill his yearning for adventure. In the days of old all dragons were free to travel the lands as they chose. However, once the darkness started to spread the council had to make new laws to ensure survival of not only their own race but that of the humans as well. To do so a pact was made between the two races, every year the dragon council would choose as many dragons as was needed to fill positions among the humans to help fight off evil, defending truth and justice. There were many positions a dragon could do, from navigator, to healer, but the warriors had the most exciting lives to Gladiair. A dragon could only be chosen in their youth as they were more likely to survive the bonding experience. Once past that age the dragons were left alone to start their own families or live a life of seclusion amongst the caverns. It surprised Gladiair how many dragons hoped for such a life style. He could never picture himself shut up in a cavern or starting a family of his own. He yearned for a life of adventure and excitement, which is why he enjoyed the company of Ashwyn and Eli. They were always talking of adventures they wanted to go on, or glorious battles they would fight in. They often flew over to the training fields and watched the warriors practice battle maneuvers in the sky, which they would try to recreate on their own. One advantage the warriors had over them was they had all the proper equipment a dragon needed to carry passengers safely in the air. Being without them, Ashwyn and Eli had to make their own provisions to stay aback him during flight. In the beginning of their friendship they had tried to tie themselves to Gladiair using ropes, but his scales were to sharp, cutting through and leaving them in a heap on the ground. Having no other choice, they learned to ride him higher up on the neck, just beneath the fringe on his head. This provided great protection from the winds as they could duck down against him and be sheltered. Their legs could also fit snuggly between the scales that moved and flexed. They wondered why other dragon riders didn't do it this way. However, since they weren't technically supposed to be riding him anyway, they had no one to ask.

"Oh Gladiair! I am so excited for you! I hope that you get bonded today. However, I am so going to miss riding you. You were our freedom." Ashwyn said.

Ashwyn hugged closely to him as she spoke, the cool air sliding across her as they flew high to the landing at the side of the mountain.

Yes, but we will always be friends. Maybe my new rider will allow you a ride from time to time. Gladiair suggested.

He secretly hoped his rider could be either Eli or Ashwyn but knew that could never happen since the human candidates also had to be chosen by the Prophet in their village and neither one had even met the man. A human could be picked at any age to be paired with a dragon. That was decided by the village prophet. Eli was the better rider out of the two if Ashwyn had to admit it. Maybe it was from his lack of eyesight, but whatever the reason his balance was impeccable. He was able now to stand upon Gladiair's back while riding, never losing his balance, whooping into the wind, even on an upward descent. Ashwyn would never brave such a move without leather tack holding her in place if she were to fall. Gladiair rumbled a laugh beneath them as they came to gentle landing.

− 2 −

They had landed on the side entrance to the caverns, not wanting to be seen flying in on Gladiair. The caverns were cut out of bright orange and yellow rocks, making it look like sunshine all the time inside. Dragons naturally loved heat and warmth, and these rocks emitted a low heat constantly making it a tad stuffy for humans but perfect for dragons.

We are going to the Upper Room. Stay behind me, hopefully you will go unnoticed until we get inside. Gladiair said.

Ashwyn once asked Gladiair why he spoke in their minds instead of out-loud. He explained dragons can speak out loud but found it beneath them and tiresome. Speaking in the mind was quicker, and could allow for visual pictures as well, making it a much more effective way to communicate. The path they were on had been completely deserted until they reached the hallway coming off the main entrance. They would have to use it to continue to the Upper Room as the floors slowly slopped upward. A large black dragon growled at them as he passed by, they were known for being aggressive and territorial. Gladiair held his own and showed no sign of being intimidated however. Ashwyn had always admired Gladiair's strong muscular build, and bravery. He had many more years to grow still but even now he was considered tall and strong for a dragon. After a group of riders went by in their emerald green uniforms with matching dragon breast plates, they took the opportunity to fall in line behind them and continue the upward climb. Eli couldn't stop smiling as he left one hand on Gladiair's hip to help navigate. Neither one of them had ever come into the caverns before, however today was a special day. Once they reached the top Ashwyn couldn't believe the ginormous round room with circular rock tiers of seats cascading back down into the mountain. On the seats sat the village elders in robes of blue, with dragons in deep reds, purples, greens and yellows spread out. The room was completely silent, no one spoke. Ashwyn spoke in her mind to Gladiair

"I thought there would be more talking" she said.

There is from the dragons. They have shields up, so the humans can't hear them.

That was a bit unnerving she thought. They found seats near the top, which was a relief seeing as how they would have been noticed for sure if they had to descend the steps lowering them to the bottom seats. At the front of the room was a throne cut out of the stone with twelve seats on each side. The large black dragon they had passed earlier was sitting on one of the twelve seats. He must be someone important she thought.

He is. That's Rogan. He's the Head of War Affairs, Gladiair explained.

Ashwyn was accustomed to Gladiair answering her questions without her asking them. He chuckled.

I promise. I only do it to you and Eli...most of the time. Other humans are much less interesting and self-absorbed to listen to.

The Queen of Dragons, Rosalyn came strutting in, her head held high. She was shorter than the black seated next to her, but her eyes showed wisdom and were piercing like an eagle. Ashwyn decided she probably didn't miss much that went on in her community, or in her village below either. Speaking in a loud, feminine voice

"Welcome to the day of the Chosen. We are pleased to have so many young candidates seeking a dragon this year. We are also proud of the dragons who have been asked to bond with these humans. The bonding process is not one to be taken lightly. Once bonded your life is forever connected with your rider and vice versa. If one of you gets injured, the injury will appears on the other as well. Also, if one of you dies, the other will also die. Your thoughts, your motives and your actions are no longer your own. It is a dangerous process, some do not survive. If there are any human candidates who feel this responsibility is too much to bear, please leave now." Rosalyn said.

Ashwyn noticed the dragons weren't mentioned and wondered why.

A dragon would never back down he or she had volunteered, that would be dishonorable. Even one chosen by the Queen would accept their fate. It is an honor to serve. Gladiair proudly responded.

"Will all the human candidates please come forward" Rosalyn instructed.

At this ten boys of various ages walked up to the front of the room, again no girls were picked. There were girl dragon riders but much fewer of them then the boys. Ashwyn knew it was because the elders felt the boys were better built and suited for battle and life in the wild. However, she strongly disagreed and hoped every year she would be picked to participate in the ceremony. As she understood it there was no formal way to volunteer in her village. The Prophet simply convened with the Elders and he somehow foretold who would make it as a rider or at least could try and become one. From there one of the Elders would visit the home of the candidate and inform the family, usually only a day or two before the Choosing was to take place. Eli wanted nothing more than to be a dragon rider, but his chances were even lower. Once bonded, whatever dragon chose him would also share in his blindness, so none ever would.

"All dragons who have been chosen, please come stand behind the candidates."

Here I go!

Gladiair stood proudly and made his way to the front of the room. He was the most beautiful yellow dragon Ashwyn had ever seen. His eyes were fierce and terrifying, yet she knew they held gentleness none but her and Eli had seen. This was his third year in a row to be picked to come before the council. However, each time, after reading the minds of the candidates he had refused to bond. A dragon was allowed to refuse three times, after that they were released and no longer allowed to participate. This was his final year and his last chance. Ashwyn didn't quite understand it, he had wanted so badly to be bonded, yet he never would tell her why he chose not to.

Some things cannot be explained was Gladiair's only reply.

For the ten human candidates there were only eight dragons. That meant two would not be chosen as riders today. The humans were always more eager to bond then the dragon race was to be bonded with them. Ashwyn couldn't blame them, she didn't care for most humans herself. One dragon after another slowly walked down the line, pausing occasionally in front of a candidate to stare right through them it seemed to Ashwyn. She wondered what it was they were looking for? Once a dragon had picked a prospective rider, the dragon would stand in front of that rider, otherwise they would continue down the line. A short ruby red dragon with black horns sticking straight up was the first to choose. He stood by a boy with long black hair braided down his back giving a slight nod, the signal he had decided on this boy. A thin green dragon slunk lazily down the line before choosing a short boy with cropped brown hair, they would probably go into the service of the healers Ashwyn thought, neither one looked very physically inclined. Gladiair was once again last to choose, he made eye contact with each candidate as he moved down the line. Ashwyn felt her palms starting to sweat as he neared the last boy in the line. She had seen him practicing out in the meadow with his brothers many times. He was muscular and tall, and no doubt would make a mighty warrior someday. With head held high however, Gladiair passed the line of candidates standing before the Queen and shaking his head, once again refusing to bond with those present. The Queen herself seemed sad, it was as if she also had hoped for Gladiair to finally be bonded and join the ranks of riders. After a pause between the two the Queen addressed the audience.

"Very well. Congratulations to all the Chosen today. The humans who have been picked by their dragons, will go with that dragon out the west corridor. The bonding process will begin shortly. Those candidates who were not chosen, thank you for your bravery, you may leave through the main entrance. Transport dragons will be waiting to take you back down to your village. All other Elders and the presiding Prophet are also welcome to watch the bonding process. Until next year" with that she gave an ear-splitting roar which bounced off the walls, joined in by other dragons.

Ashwyn and Eli rose to leave when a hand suddenly was placed on their shoulder. Looking up into the face of a middle-aged man, with a grey beard, salt and pepper hair, and stern blue eyes. Judging by his elaborate blue robe there was no doubt he was the Prophet.

"You two, will come with me" he stated very sternly.

Ashwyn's heart started to pound in her chest, what trouble would they be in for coming to the Choosing. Maybe she should explain to him that they were invited by Gladiair. She frantically looked around for their friend, how did she lose sight of the giant yellow dragon. He was nowhere to be seen as dragons and humans exited out of the room. The man in the robe took them to a door found at the west side of the cavern. It was only large enough for a human to fit through. Ashwyn panicked thinking of all the horrible things that could be inside as punishment and also realizing Gladiair would never fit through the door to come rescue them. Eli seemed much calmer as he held casually onto Ashwyns hand as she led him along next to her. Not that she needed to, the man still had his hands on their shoulders pushing them forward.

-3-

Once inside the room she could see all the dragons that had chosen to be bonded were sitting with their soon to be riders kneeling before them. This must be the bonding ceremony. She thought excitedly. Why would they be allowed to witness such a sacred event? Only very few humans were ever allowed to watch it, and since her and Eli weren't elders or Prophets she stood puzzled and confused. She looked up to the man behind her in the blue robe, he kept his gaze steadily forward and refused to make eye contact. What were they waiting for? Gladiair finally walked into the room through a much larger entrance, that must have been how the dragons came in. He went and stood in the circle of those to be bonded, but no rider stood before him. He refused to speak to Ashwyn or Eli in their minds, keeping his gaze steadily forward as the other dragons did. A loud roar was once again heard bouncing down the cavern as Queen Rosalyn entered the room. She paused a moment to look over those present, then turned and made her way over to Ashwyn, Eli and the man in the blue robe. She was much scarier in person, Ashwyn felt suddenly sick to her stomach. Taking a moment to glance over at Eli he had gone pale and was staring down at the floor. Even without vision he was intimated by her presence.

You two have caused quite the disturbance today. Rosalyn's feminine voice echoed in Ashwyns mind and must have in Elis also as he jumped suddenly.

No other dragon besides Gladiair had ever spoken to them. The man in the blue robe must have heard it as well.

The man in the blue robe introduced her. "This is Ashwyn, daughter of Prophet Violet and Prophet Seth."

Ashwyn couldn't believe what she was hearing. Prophet? No one had ever told her that her parents were prophets. Eli seemed equally as surprised by this new piece of information.

"This over here is Eli, of the Wild Horse People" he said.

Rosalyn looked at each one for a long period of time, no doubt reading their minds Ashwyn thought. She heard a light laugh like running water echo once again in her mind.

The mind is not the only thing a dragon can see inside of a person. Thank you Prophet Islan for the introductions. It seems, against tradition, and sound reason, Eli, you have also been Chosen today by a dragon. A very stubborn, brave, dragon, Rosalyn said.

Ashwyn couldn't believe what she was hearing. Eli had been CHOSEN! By Gladiair! Without first being approved by the village elders. That had never happened before. Had it?

It is unusual, but it has been done. Rosalyn continued. *Do you accept this invitation?* She waited for a reply.

Eli was beaming as he replied "Yes. I accept."

I thought you might. Rosalyn said.

Was she smiling? Ashwyn couldn't tell.

The road ahead will not be easy for you and Gladiair. We are still not sure if he will go blind from the bonding process. He insists he wants to try anyway. If so I do not know what your lives will be like. Being bonded to a human is hard enough for a dragon, let alone one with a disability. That has not been done. I do know Gladiair however. He has a mighty spirit and is made like dragons of old. I do not doubt him. I have allowed this only because this is his last year to bond, by dragon law. If you agree, you may be killed in the process. Do you still accept?

Eli paused for a moment, surprising Ashwyn. She turned to look at him, he was staring directly ahead of him to where Gladiair stood, almost as if he could see him. "Gladiair has always believed in me. He has taught me more from his friendship then anyone ever could. I would not wish to force blindness upon him."

Gladiairs strong voice suddenly entered the conversation. Had he been listening all along? *You are not choosing me. It is I, who am choosing you. Accept Eli. We will be fine.*

With those words of encouragement, Eli stood straighter and finally said "I agree".

Speaking for the entire room to hear. "Very well. Please make your way to stand before your dragon."

A large green dragon entered the room with kind brown eyes. Eli made his way carefully with staff in hand towards Gladiair. Ashwyn was so happy for her friends, although a little disappointed she had not also been chosen. She pushed thoughts out of her mind of jealousy, or grief at them living far off on adventures without her, and instead tried to focus on how happy she was for them.

Prophet Islan remained beside her, no longer holding onto her shoulder. "Not many get to witness such a sacred ritual" adding importance to the moment.

The dragon speaking was a female she could tell from the way she spoke. "We will now begin the bonding process. Future Dragon Riders kneel before your dragon and repeat after me. Where there is injustice we swear to bring justice. Where there is evil we swear to do good. Where there is weakness we swear to be strong. When you need me I will be there. When I need you, I can depend on you. Two lives, becoming one, in this life, and the next."

Ashwyn's mind was racing, was this really happening? She hadn't even had time to stop and think.

The ceremony continued, "dragons, prepare to bathe your riders with fire" the green dragon said. This was the dangerous part.

Ashwyn had heard stories of dragons who were unable to separate their fires. All dragons had two fires, one for defense to scorch and kill and another to heal. They would need to use their healing fire to heal the weakness and darkness inside of their rider, so they would be pure enough to bond with their dragon. Somehow by using this fire, it allowed for the two souls to be joined as one, while the green dragon continued to recite a prayer over them. Gladiair slowly drew his breathe in, looking at Eli intently as he prepared to bath him, with his mouth opening wider then Ashwyn had ever seen. Out of instinct she looked quickly over at Eli and was surprised to see him smiling, looking directly back into Gladiairs mouth. She wanted to warn him to shut his eyes but there was no time. Fires in all the different colors of the rider's present started to engulf the humans before them. Ashwyn was horrified to hear a scream at the other end of the room. The red had not been able to separate his fire, with his future rider ending in a pile of ash before him. The other dragons seemed to be doing fine and no one else was screaming at least. The fires seemed to last a long time, until finally they started to die out, leaving the room slightly cooler than it had been. Ashwyn wanted to run up and check on her friends, however Prophet Islan held her in place once again.

The green dragon spoke "Rise. You are now bonded forever with the dragon in front of you. The two of you must learn to work and live together. Each pair will be leaving in the morning with an escort to the Ancient Islands. I suggest you take the time ahead of you to pack what you will need and say goodbye to your families. You well remain on the Islands until it is determined you are ready to assume a post, the time varies for each pair and cannot be determined at this time. Consider yourselves blessed, this bond is rare, and precious, respect it."

The Queen and green dragon strode out of the room side by side, followed by the rest of the riders who must have been mind speaking with their dragons. Gladiair and Eli looked over at Ashwyn. She was finally released by Prophet Islan and allowed to run up to them. She was so excited she grabbed Eli right away and threw him into a hug.

"Easy Ashwyn, I've never seen you so flushed" Eli said.

Wait. What? Ashwyn couldn't' believe what she heard. She pushed Eli arm's length away to look at him, and found him staring right back at her, looking her directly in the eyes.

"You can see?!" She couldn't believe it.

They both broke out in laughter as he let his staff fall to the ground. Glancing up at Gladiair to find he was also smiling back down, or what they would assume a dragon would look like if he was smiling.

See. I told you it would be fine, Gladiair said.

He was pretty smug even for a dragon.

Rosalyn wasn't sure it could be done, but I had heard of a dragon who used his healing fire to correct human disabilities. I always felt in my heart that I was meant to bond with Eli. It took the Queen many years to convince, and until I knew for sure I didn't want to raise anyone's hopes.

Looking at Ashwyn now Gladiair said *Do not be disappointed. I think you'll find your fate will always be interwind with ours.*

Ashwyn looked up at him questioningly but before she could speak Prophet Islan interrupted. "That was risky. Even for a very brave dragon and blind boy. I will be your escort to the Ancient Islands in the morning. Ashwyn, you will be accompanying us also. You will ride with me on Thunder." Ashwyn's mind was racing in all directions "but I haven't been chosen. I thought only riders got to leave?"

Without further explanation he stated, "they do. Use the hours ahead to collect your things and say goodbye to your families. Gladiair will have you both back here tomorrow at first light" and he walked away, blue robes flowing behind him.

- 4 -

Mounting onto Gladiair at the entrance the trio could not have been more excited how the day had turned out. It was well past noon now that they had come out of the caverns. Below in the village the town was celebrating with music and dancing. Gladiair was making a straight line to Ashwyns cottage however where she had always lived with her Aunt Letti. Letti was standing outside of the cottage working on her rose garden as they landed. Letti had the build of a warrior and practiced daily her combat skills and training. Ashwyn couldn't remember her parents and Letti spoke of them very rarely. She had been left there when she was a toddler, for her safety is the only reason she was ever given. Letti had always been kind to her, teaching her how to use various weapons, which herbs in the forest were safe to eat, reading and writing, and the value of cooking, which Ashwyn still hadn't begun to master.

I'll take Eli to his people of the Wild Horses. We will be back to get you before first light tomorrow, and then, the real adventures begin! Gladiair was always up for anything exciting.

Ashwyn climbed down and stood waving at them as flew off west of her little brown stone cottage with the dark green door. Eli's tribe lived just beyond the grassy hills in the meadow. The Wild Horse People stayed in colorful tents of bright reds, oranges and yellows. A nomadic tribe, they would set up camp at various places around the meadow, letting the grass grow back where it had been tromped down by their feet and that of the horses they took care of. It took

Ashwyn a good hour to reach his camp during the summer months when the tribe set up their tents along the forest tree line. She could often smell the scent of the exotic dishes they cooked with strong spices of cayenne, cumin, or cabbage. They seemed to make a lot of cabbage she always thought. Ashwyn continued to watch Gladiair and Eli fly until they were out of sight before turning and running back to tell Letti all about what had happened. Letti held up her hand as Ashwyn approached, which halted Ashwyn in her steps.

"Prophet Islan has already been by" Letti looked defeated and much older than Ashwyn thought. "I had hoped we would have more time. I wanted to prepare you more for what was ahead. I am so sorry Ashwyn, your time however has come to leave the safety I can provide."

Ashwyn didn't really understand what her Aunt was talking about. She had never felt unsafe. Letti seemed so sad and discouraged, not at all as happy as Ashwyn would have imagined. They said very little for the rest of the evening. They had lived a mostly reclusive life in their cottage at the edge of the village, preferring the peace of nature opposed to the bustle of the crowds. That night they ate a simple meal in their cottage, afterwards Letti reminded Ashwyn she would need to pack and handed her a brown leather bag to place her things in.

"Prophet Islan said my parents were also prophets. Is that true Aunt Letti?" Ashwyn asked.

Letti froze on her way to her room, without turning around "Yes, they were. Very powerful Prophets." She said and went on into her room, shutting the door behind her.

Ashwyn packed a couple pair of leggings and tunics, the dragon silver hair clip left to her by her mother, a brown cloak, her short sword, and laid her bow and arrow quiver across the bag. She went to sleep that night dreaming of dragons, and prophets, and wondering why she was being allowed to tag along. Maybe Gladiair had insisted since they were all good friends. The thoughts swirling around in her mind left her with little sleep, which turned out to be a good thing because she didn't want to over sleep and have Gladiair and Eli waiting on her. Dressing in the dark, placing her bow and arrows over her shoulder and grabbing her leather bag, she made her way down the wooden staircase to the kitchen. She was trying to decide if she needed to pack food or not when Letti came in from the front door with Prophet Islan following behind her. He was no longer wearing his elaborate blue robe, but instead wore black travel clothes and matching cloak. His long salt and pepper hair was braided down his back and he looked much younger then he had the day before.

"Change of plans. We will be leaving directly from here to the Ancient Islands." Prophet Islan said.

Ashwyn was startled by the sudden change of plans. She had only ever seen the Prophet in the village about important affairs or riding back and forth to the caverns on his mighty blue dragon, after he had been gone for long periods. On those rare occasions he had never once spoken to her and now he was standing in her kitchen, before dawn. She looked to Letti for explanation.

"It is no longer safe for you to stay here. You must leave now" Letti said.

Grabbing Ashwyn up in a quick hug she took her hand and hurried her out the front door carrying her bag as she threw it to Prophet Islan. Thunder was just as big as Gladiair, and much less friendly.

Prophet Islan said "Given the circumstances" looking over at Gladiair who looked sheepishly up to the sky. "I will assume you already know how to mount and ride on a dragon."

Ashwyn slowly climbed up along Thunders front leg, holding

onto his wing as she threw herself in the saddle in front of Prophet Islan.

"You may call me Islan by the way" he said.

He spoke these words in a much kinder voice, as he showed her how to strap herself in. She waved to Letti as they took off, with Gladiair following behind them. Ashwyn knew that once a dragon was bonded they only spoke to their rider through the mind but decided to check and see if Gladiair would still speak with her. He had yesterday after all.

Of course, I will still speak with you. We will always be friends Ashwyn. I will speak to whom I choose. Gladiair said.

She was relieved, it made her feel much less isolated from the group. As they passed over the mountain, she looked around for the other dragons and their new riders.

"I thought the other riders were flying to the Ancient Islands also?" She yelled back at Islan behind her.

"They will be, they will leave at first light, we didn't have time to wait for them" Islan shouted back.

Ashwyn was starting to get concerned, she asked Gladiair why they couldn't wait.

Gladiair explained. *Thunder says we are in danger, that evil is tracking us, but he won't tell me why. He said not to worry and focus on my flying.*

"How long until we get to the Ancient Islands?" She asked behind her once again to Islan.

"A few days" he said.

Seeing as how she wasn't going to get much information out of him, she decided to enjoy the ride instead. Looking down, they were far past the mountain meadows where she had grown up. Dragons could fly incredibly fast and already they were crossing large rocky areas heading out to the sea glistening far in the distance. The sun had risen to noon as they started to descended landing next to a crystal-clear lake.

Another party is landing behind us. Gladiair spoke just as Ashwyn and Eli turned to watch a group of dark green dragons descending next to them.

Islan stepped passed Thunder who lumbered to the lake to get a drink and waited for the riders to dismount. The riders were all wearing matching green uniforms to match their dragons, that shifted color in the sunlight. The dragons were snorting and growling towards Gladiair and Thunder in a display of territory, these were dragon scouts, and this was probably a regular landing place for them. Ashwyn walked over to Eli who was studying a colony of ants closely near the rocks.

"What are you doing?" She crouched down to see what he was looking at.

Eli said "do you know, in my memories, I could never remember what ants looked like. It's amazing how hard they work, and they are so tiny. Look at them! Carrying that giant leaf, it'll take them half of the day to get it back down that hole."

Ashwyn studied Eli thinking how grateful she was for her friend. He could finally see again! After all these years. With all the excitement it was easy to forget that this miracle had happened right before her. "You were really courageous for bonding! You could have been killed!"

Ashwyn knew that she would have made the same decision if she were him though. Eli shrugged in his usual playful manner and turned to face Islan and the Commander of the greens speaking heatedly to one another

"Wonder what that's about?" He said motioning towards the debate.

They are arguing. The Commander wants us to turn back and go back to the meadows. Islan thinks the man is an arrogant fool. I think Islan is winning though, he is higher ranking.

Gladiair had his back turned towards the feud getting a drink next to Thunder, making Ashwyn assume this was one of those times Gladiair chose to listen to the men's minds as well. Islan came back to join their party calm and collected as he set about gathering sticks to build a fire. Once the fire was assembled Thunder lumbered back over and lite it, using much more flame then was necessary, probably in a display to intimidate the smaller greens still standing off by themselves. Gladiair sat smugly down behind Eli and Ashwyn as Islan produced granola, sweet bread, and fruits for them all, including the dragons.

"Eat up, and then we will ride onto the seashores before stopping for the night. The greens" he said with an irritated tone "we'll continue on with us as far as the sea" Islan said.

Eli wondered out loud, "they looked as though they were headed in the direction of the meadows, why would they turn around and go back the way they just came?"

Islan stopped eating to look over the group, "because I told them to," and he continued eating.

Ashwyn had a question of her own "Islan, why was I brought along, when I am not a dragon rider?"

Even saying it out-loud she could hear the disappointment in her voice and regretted not speaking with more confidence.

"You are not a dragon rider" Islan stated "only because you do not have a dragon. Once you have a dragon. Then you will become a dragon rider".

That made no sense to her at all. Looking at the rest of the groups reaction told her that none of the others understood it either. "You mean I'm going to have a dragon? I thought all the young dragons lived in the caverns by the meadow? Why wasn't I allowed to bond yesterday?"

As if he didn't hear her Islan continued. "Alright" he slapped his legs and kicked out the fire "back up we go!"

He did seem in much brighter spirits since leaving the meadows. The outdoors seemed to suite Islan more than being in the caverns Upper Rooms handling affairs.

Thunder says Islan hates having to keep peace constantly between the humans and dragons. He would much rather spend all his time flying and exploring, but being a Prophet, that is not an option for him until retirement. Gladiair said.

Ashwyn thought poor Islan, having to serve when he didn't want to, she almost wondered if that was like slavery.

It is not. Everyone needs and has a purpose. He is fulfilling his. Nothing lasts forever, once he has completed his duty to the Elders and Queen, he will find a new purpose. Gladiair always knew exactly the right answer and they always sounded so wise.

Eli bounced up onto Gladiair so quickly he was mounted before Islan had all the supplies strapped back onto Thunder.

"Have you noticed any differences to your vision since the bonding?" Islan asked in Eli's direction as he continued to fill the saddle bags with the extra water skins he had just finished filling.

Eli thought for a moment. "Well, sometimes when I'm looking at someone, or something, like the ants, I can see something about them. It's weird, like a halo of colors surrounding them, only each has its own color and I think it means something, but I'm not sure what."

Islan shook his head in a gesture indicating he knew exactly what he met. "What you are seeing, is the way Gladiair sees. A dragon does not just see a living being, he sees what kind of person he is by the colors that radiates around him. Great evil will be surrounded in darkness for example, great good will be surrounded in white light. Those are the two easiest to decipher. The other colors each have their own meaning but are much more complicated to understand. Gladiair will be able to help you with that. I wondered if that would happen, your dragon shared so much of himself to heal you, you'll pry find you've acquired more dragon manners then you realize" he said the last part almost smiling.

Ashwyn once again felt a bit jealous that Gladiair and Eli had become so much closer so quickly and she was starting to feel like the third one out. An image flashed in her mind of a young white dragon with opalescent scales and bright blue eyes searching constantly. The dragon looked exhausted at first but perked up as if she had suddenly recognized something she was looking for.

Gladiair was that one of your memories? She sent her question to him through their mental link.

Gladiair replied. *It was not, but I saw it as well, so did Eli. I do not recognize that dragon. She must be a wild one. Why we saw her though…..I do not know. Perhaps we should ask Islan?*

Ashwyn would rather not sound crazy to Islan, he seemed so wise and serious, she shrugged it off and soon forgot about it altogether as Thunder lifted off his giant blue legs propelling them off the ground in a cat like jump.

− 5 −

The day was bright, and the air was fresh and clean. The air around the meadow always smelled of pine and earth, rich and dark. The air this far away was starting to smell salty and invigorating, telling them they were getting closer to the water. Thunders large body was harder for Ashwyn to gain her balance on. Putting her legs wider apart then she was used to on Gladiair. However, since she was strapped in there was really no need for her to hold on, she only did so out of habit. She knew that Islan would be working with Thunder mentally to plot their course, and Thunder would be showing Islan ahead of time what maneuvers he would be making, they worked together as a team, as did all dragon riders. No reins were needed to steer a dragon like the ground men used on their horses. In fact, reins were considered belittling to a dragon and they would never allow themselves to be steered like a dumb animal. Dragons were thinking, intelligent beings, more than capable of taking care of themselves. It was a privilege that they allowed her weaker race to ride them and be part of their lives. She felt that the dragons offered humans much more than a human could ever hope to offer a dragon. Ashwyn knew not all humans thought that way, but she also knew that they should.

"Hold tight" Islan barked into her ear startling Ashwyn from her day dreams.

A hoard of orange bird like dragons chasing after them with large screeching pointed beaks. Bright silver armor was attached along their wings and covering a cone shape on their heads, these birds had reins in their mouth and evil looking black shadows with black hoods covering them riding atop their backs. Ashwyn had never seen anything so horrifying in her life. She wondered if these were the pterodactyls she had heard Gladiair tell stories about. If so they were a merciless species who attacked for no reason and held no honor.

"Who are they?" She yelled back.

Islan didn't answer as Thunder started to climb higher and higher. Gladiair was trying to keep up as he pushed his wings harder and harder to gain altitude. None of them besides Islan and Thunder were used to flying this high up past the clouds. Ashwyn was starting to feel light headed and Gladiair wasn't speaking in her mind anymore when she called to him. She could see he was still flying however the strain must have been hard on him not allowing him to keep contact. The dark green dragons who were accompanying them from behind started to fan out creating a circle around them. The dark greens took turns shooting green flames at the Oranges below them hitting three sending them spiraling out of control to the ground. Three more continued to climb although Ashwyn could see they kept trying to retreat but their riders wouldn't let them. The oranges pterodactyls were much lighter than the dragons making them gain ground more quickly however the dragons were better defended with their scales and the fact they could breathe fire.

We are also far more intelligent. Gladiair finally chimed in.

"Now!" Islan yelled to who she wasn't sure as he grabbed her around the waist and Thunder suddenly flipped head down going into a deep spiral spinning like a top towards the ground below at an alarming rate. Ashwyn almost thought about throwing up but slowly slipped unconscious, certain she was about to die.

Where are you? The voice of the white dragon spoke.

Ashwyn heard the words in her mind, picturing the same small white dragon with bright blue eyes looking directly at her. The dragon was no longer flying in the clouds, it looked like she was surrounded by boulders, with her wings outstretched, crouching down as if she were about to jump but hadn't yet. Was she talking to me? Ashwyn wondered. Her mind was throbbing and hurting, had she died on Thunder? If she had died why did she feel like she was bumping around erratically? This wasn't as peaceful as she had imagined it would be. Her eyes opened to see the large spikes sticking out around Thunders large head and Islan was still holding her around the middle.

"Wake up!" she heard Islan barking at her, "you need to hold yourself upright".

Suddenly Ashwyn realized she had flopped forward in the saddle like a rag doll. Bracing her hands before her she pulled herself back into a sitting position. She still felt light headed as shots of pain kept pulsing through her head turning her vision black. The pterodactyls and their riders continued to screech from underneath them as their riders held their hands above their heads as if they were going to grab onto the dragons from below. That seemed ridiculous to Ashwyn until Gladiair explained.

They are druids, they are trying to bring us down by black magic.

Islan's leather straps went slack as he unbuckled himself, throwing his cloak to the side and standing up. He moved gracefully running along the top of Thunder shooting arrows back down at the druids. How he managed not to fall off was astonishing to Ashwyn. He looked much like Eli did when he stood on Gladiair for fun back home, but going much faster, with evil men trying to kill them, made it seem much more impressive. Islan was able to shoot two more down as Gladiair lost patience, dropping down behind the last bird and flaming it in bright yellow flames. The bird caught fire screeching as it turned to ash. Thunder turned and growled back at Gladiair, as he slowed coming right up next to them. Islan jumped back into his spot behind Ashwyn, buckling his straps

"How are you feeling?" Islan inquired.

Ashwyn seemed to be the only one who was fighting to stay conscious and she couldn't figure out why. Feeling embarrassed to admit it, but realizing she probably needed help.

"My head really hurts, and my vision, it keeps blacking out" she finally admitted.

"We need to land" Islan ordered.

Thunder flew a short time more over grey boulders until he slipped between two rocky cliffs and landed in the bowl-shaped crater. Gladiair landed much less gracefully skidding into the rocks, panting and puffing smoke through his nose. Eli slid down and went to the front of Gladiair, probably checking to see if he was alright Ashwyn decided as she looked around them for the dark greens.

"Where are the green riders?" She asked as Islan unstrapped her and helped her slide down the leg of Thunder.

"The druids got them" Islan growled.

"Got them?" She asked "what do you mean got them? How does a pterodactyl kill a dragon?"

"The birds don't, it's their riders the druids. They absorb their victim into themselves through dark magic. The greens refused to let me put up protection shields around them before we left. It was too late by the time we were under attack. Thunder tried but they were too stubborn, too arrogant to listen." Islan grumbled.

What a horrible way to die Ashwyn thought as she stumbled and Islan lowered her to the ground.

"Sit still" he rummaged through his leather saddle bag until he produced a white vial of some glittering liquid. "Here drink this. It will help clear your mind."

Willing to do anything at this point to feel better she took a sip. It was sweet and cold, taking only a few moments before she started to feel better. Islan looked drawn and worried, staring at her as if he expected her to crumple and explode.

Eli walked over "you okay?"

She gave a nod and as best a smile as she could. "How come no one else got sick?" She asked anyone who would answer.

Eli shrugged and looked over at Islan who was still kneeling on the ground next to Ashwyn studying her.

"Because, Eli is not a Prophet, and I had my shield up. It should have been enough to protect you as well. For some reason, it didn't" Islan pondered.

Eli looked curiously over at Ashwyn "are you saying that Ashwyn is a Prophet like you?"

Ashwyn laughed out loud, that sounded absurd. She was no Prophet she was certain. A Prophet was someone who prayed often and saw revelations, they were given special powers to help people like heal them and read their minds, tell what their futures would hold, which is why the Prophets chose the candidates for dragon riders.

"Just because you do not pray, does not mean you are not a Prophet" Islan retorted.

Had he just read her mind? Ashwyn thought nervously.

"Unfortunately, now the druids also know what you are. I was hoping to make it to the Ancient Islands without running into them. They have spread further south than they normally are. We won't be safe staying here for the night. As soon as Thunder is through disciplining Gladiair, we will mount up and fly as quick as we can towards the Islands." Islan declared.

Discipling Gladiair? Ashwyn wondered for what he could possibly be in trouble for. He had saved them from the last pterodactyl after all.

"That's the problem" Eli looked sheepishly over to Ashwyn as he said, "we were told not to flame them. Apparently, the druids can absorb a dragon's fire and use it against that dragon. A dragon is usually immune to other dragon's fire, but their own......would kill them."

Ashwyn had never heard that before, but then again, how would a dragon ever flame itself besides maybe a tail or scorched foot perhaps. Eli continued "Gladiair got impatient and a tad over confident".

Islan smiled before giving a roaring laugh that surprised them all. "It was a completely foolish thing to do, but it saved our hides, so for that, I for one am grateful".

Thunder gave a disapproving look in Islans direction, then decided to give up on his internal lecture with Gladiair apparently as he turned waiting to be mounted once again. Gladiair followed his actions and turned to face the opening as they waited for the humans to pass around the water skin before they all got back into their saddles and tethered themselves back into place. Ashwyn continued to argue with herself that she was absolutely not a Prophet. Somehow the druids must have mistaken her for someone else and Islan must be confused.

"I am not confused, nor will I ever be God willing" Islan calmly replied in her ear.

Ashwyn was at once embarrassed and could feel her cheeks starting to turn bright red.

You look as red as a tomato.

Gladiair laughed at her through their connection and she could also see Eli smiling. Looking at Eli riding on the back of Gladiair with his dark brown hair flying in the wind gave him a wild look. Knowing that her friend could now see everything that she could see was still hard to wrap her mind around. Remembering what Eli had said about people giving off halos of color around them she wondered what color they now saw around her.

Your light is white. It has always been bright white. That is how I knew I could trust you as a friend. Gladiair confirmed.

Bright white? Wasn't that the color that Islan said was the color of great good?

Yes.

I didn't feel greatly good inside, in fact, more times than not I find myself struggling with dark thoughts trying to prove to myself that I am not dark inside.

Gladiair responded, "*that is how you know you are good. Bad people never struggle within themselves to find goodness and truth.*"

"Gladiair is right. Think over your childhood" Islan joined in the conversation out loud.

Great she thought, could everyone besides Eli read her mind now? Islan and Gladiair both laughed out loud.

"Yes, for now at least. When we get to the Islands. I will show you how to put a shield over your mind, so no one can listen to your thoughts. However, for now, you are vulnerable to our eavesdropping I'm afraid" Islan sounded more like a kind grandfather now giving advice then the barking military warrior from hours before.

Bringing her thoughts back under control, Ashwyn started to play moments back from her childhood. I guess there were times when she had lost a special item, like the hair clip her mother had left her, and after looking without finding it, she would suddenly see a flash in her mind of the exact spot it was in. Or when she was trying to mediate and pray with Letti and suddenly she would picture Eli and know exactly what he was doing. She always assumed those were just day dreams though and never asked to find out if they were true or not. If she had been born a Prophet, why hadn't Letti told her, her Aunt would have surely known.

A loud sigh came from behind her "she does know" Islan sounded almost regretful for saying the words out loud. "She was trying to protect you, she wouldn't let me train you. Letti felt that if you didn't practice your skill it would somehow save you from your fate. Unfortunately, or fortunately that is not how life works."

Everyone has a purpose. That was one of Gladiairs favorite sayings as he repeated it again to her now.

Ashwyn didn't know if she should be upset with Letti or not. She decided that Letti loved her very much and was doing what she truly felt was the right thing.

That's another reason why you should know that you are good. You seek to find the good in others. Gladiair was a good friend, and always had believed in her and Eli both.

She wondered if it was because he saw more in them, then she ever saw. Coming swiftly up to the shoreline Ashwyn could see out over the ocean. The view made her hold her breathe as she gazed into the deep blue waters below. The sun reflected off of it warming the under bellies of the dragons. Waves splashed up and rolled passed as tiny birds flew all around them. An image of the white dragon came into Ashwyns mind as clear as if she were standing right before them.

Slow down, I can't keep up!

Ashwyn was starting to take it more seriously now, she decided to tell Islan. "Islan I think we should slow down" She shouted back behind her, so he could hear her over the roaring waves below.

"Like heck we are slowing down. Those druids will be on our tail by now, if we slow down we will run right back into them, and I don't particularly care for the idea of fighting them above water" Islan retorted.

"No, it's not that" Ashwyn was starting to feel desperate "I keep having these….visions. There's a dragon and she's trying to find us, but I don't think she can for some reason."

Islan growled "For goodness sake, is she white?"

Ashwyn gasped! "Yes! How did you know that?"

"Because that is YOUR dragon. Where is she now?" Islan demanded.

Ashwyn didn't know, she told him she had only seen her a couple times over the past day and didn't take it seriously until now.

"Picture her in your mind" he instructed.

Ashwyn had to close her eyes to bring the white dragon back into her thoughts. "Now, ask her where she is" That sounded almost too easy. It wasn't as if by just picturing this dragon she didn't know she could actually speak to her.

Actually, you can, I'm just passing the shoreline now. I fear the druids will catch up to me soon. I was able to fly past a group unnoticed. They seemed disorganized, but I'm sure that will pass soon enough.

"She's just passing the shoreline!" Ashwyn sounded a bit more panicked then she had planned to.

Thunder instantly started climbing above the water back into the clouds. O great, Ashwyn thought, now I'll pass out again. This time however she didn't, surprisingly.

"You didn't pass out from flying" Islan corrected her "you passed out from the druids trying to read your mind. You did well for not being trained. You were trying to protect yourself, without knowing it. In the process you blacked yourself out, which was best really. A druid can't read the mind of an unconscious person."

Interesting she thought. The clouds were beautiful puffs of white below them and the sun was starting to set making it look like they were flying right over the sun. Gladiaiar's scales had never sparkled so brightly, Ashwyn admired his beauty as they flew on into the night.

Thunder rolled slowly turning backwards, before stretching out taking them back towards the beach. Gladiair sent a mental picture of Thunder, with wings outstretched to protect a small white dragon, with the word *family*. They stopped a hovered high above the clouds. The wings from the dragons pumped slowly, sending their bodies up and down. They could barely see the water below. Ashwyn only caught glimpses of it in between breaks as the clouds drifted by. Gladiair explained to her and Eli that they were waiting for the white dragon to go by, so she could join their group flying towards the Ancient Island.

"There!" Ashwyn pointed to an opalescent white dragon skimming low against the water. Thunder dropped down like a rock situating himself, so he would glide down behind her. Gladiair and Eli drifted alongside the small white dragon. Gladiair was much longer, and Thunder was a beast compared to her compact shape. Gladiair sent a mental picture of a small horse to Ashwyn and Eli.

I'm glad I caught up with you. The white dragon said for only Ashwyn to hear.

-6-

As the stars started to come out the dragons and their riders all started to feel the toll from the day. Especially Gladiaiar and his two friends, as they were not accustomed to flying all day and into the night. Islan and Thunder seemed to have new found energy from reserves Ashwyn couldn't imagine. The white dragon had remained mostly silent, she seemed exhausted and kept dropping dangerously close to the ocean waters. Thunder continued to fly behind her and every once in a while, would place his head underneath her back end to lift her up.

Islan must have sensed Ashwyn's concern, he tried to comfort her by saying "I think you will find this white dragon of yours to be more than a match for the druids who follow us, and by the way, her name, is Amarisk"

"You know her name?" Ashwyn didn't think to ask before if Islan knew her or not, it never occurred to her that he might. She was constantly underestimating him.

"Ummmm, yes, and she was supposed to stay on the Ancient Islands" he said. As if she would also be getting a lecture from Thunder once they all arrived just as Gladiair had not so long before.

Thunder and Islan were a respected duo and had fought in many battles together. Islan was the oldest of the Prophets and Thunder was just as old as the Queen Rosalyn herself. They were rarely at the village though, and she wasn't sure where they spent most of their time, or what all of their duties entailed. Having just turned twelve most of her life had been spent either with Letti studying, praying, meditating, or running off with Eli to explore or ride with Gladiair. She wasn't accustomed to hearing about the grown-ups duties or where the warriors came and went. Come to think of it, all she knew was that they fought for the truth and goodness, protecting those less fortunate from evil. She didn't even know exactly who the foes were that they fought unless Gladiair told them stories he had heard from the other dragons. She supposed that perhaps she had lived a rather sheltered life up until now. Finding herself being pursued by magical druids with the oldest and most respected Prophet from her village seemed bizarre enough, add to the mix that Eli had been healed of his blindness and bonded with Gladiair and it almost seemed like maybe she was dreaming or hallucinating. A screech tearing through the night sky sent terror down her spine. Gladiair quickly picked up his pace to fly beside Thunder. Thunder took his massive body, placed it over Amarisk, and grabbed her by her tail with his claws. Where her head was moments before in front of them, was now facing backwards. Her wings were useless in this position. Ashwyn watched as Amarisk gratefully closed her wings and allowed Thunder to carry her on like an infant. In unison Thunder and Gladiair shot flames of blue and yellow straight ahead of them in three fire balls, one after the other.

Warning signals. Gladiair told Ashwyn and Eli through their shared link.

Suddenly they dropped lower just in time, as bright red flames came bursting into the night air, flying over their heads followed by over twenty red dragons with their riders charging back towards the Druids on orange mounts. It was an impressive display lighting up the night sky and shining through the waters below. Relief filled Ashwyn and peace settled over her as she recognized land ahead of her. Finally, they would be safe. Thunder and Gladiair arrived at what she assumed was the Ancient Islands although in the dark she could only make out the white sands of the beach. Dozens of Riders were gathered along the beach making room for them to land.

"Should we take cover? Won't we be visible to the Druids standing on the beach like this?" Ashwyn asked Islan.

"The Ancient Islands are surrounded by an invisible protective force. Only those who wear the pendant may enter" Islan confirmed. Holding up a silver necklace that had been hidden beneath his riding tunic, on it hung a cross. "I gave Eli his when we stopped by the crater. You will also receive one after you have been bonded to your dragon. Speaking of which…."

His voice trailed off as he scanned the beach for the opalescent dragon. Thunder must have laid her down on the beach before he landed himself. "Amarisk must of went to hide. Probably embarrassed for having to be carried home. Not exactly the dignified hero she probably imagined when she set off after us" Islan explained.

I think she might be hiding. Gladiair stifled a laugh and was quickly growled at again by Thunder.

No doubt he was the very reason that she was hiding. Ashwyn closed her eyes and tried to see where Amarisk was hiding. She saw nothing but blackness before turning perplexed back to Islan.

"Can't find her, can you?" Islan didn't even look at her as he grabbed his satchel off Thunders saddle. She shook her head no. "That's because, you have a very special dragon. She has some surprises of her own, one of which, is invisibility. Although she can't control it very well. It usually only kicks in when she's afraid, or embarrassed." Islan said.

Ashwyn had never heard of a dragon going invisible before. Gladiair confirmed that he hadn't either. Thunder only seemed to be rolling his eyes in annoyance. A group of older riders approached Islan and greeted him warmly. He started walking off with them as he gestured for Eli and Ashwyn to follow. Thunder and Gladiair walked nobly behind them as they paraded up the hill and over the grassy bank. Sitting on the hill was a castle larger than anything Ashwyn could have imagined being possible. It looked smooth in the moonlight like it had been cut out of one giant piece of stone or maybe pearl. Was it possible a pearl could be so big? It would easily house all of the dragons present on the island with room to spare for the riders. Walking through the main entrance the walls were all lit with bright amethyst crystals making a shocking contrast against the white polished walls.

"This way to the dragon's sleeping chambers" Islan said. He continued to be in the lead of the riders. They walked through the other people and dragons who had waited for them to land on the beach. Other than a few glances in their direction, no one seemed surprised by their grand arrival. Once they entered into the castle the walkways gradually inclined upwards, much as they did back in the caverns to get to the upper rooms. The castle was clean, quiet and a bit dark, as if everyone had gone to bed. Ashwyn thought it made sense for the dragon's chambers to be higher up. They could probably fly straight out of their rooms this way. Once at the top of the walkway they were inside of a giant chamber with carvings of every color dragon imaginable lining the walls clear up into the ceiling. The carvings were spaced out far enough to make out each one and surrounded with flowers and vines as they climbed up towards a glass roof, where the stars shone brightly down upon them. Thunder walked passed the new comers and went straight to a cave near the back.

"That is Thunders cave. I'll go and unload him. Gladiair yours is right across from his next to the carving of a yellow dragon. Eli he is your dragon now, you will be responsible for his care from here on out. I expect you to unsaddle him, rinse him off with the watering hose attached to the wall in his chamber, make sure he has plenty of water and hay to lay on. Food well be brought to him by the stable master shortly. Understood?" Islan had his military voice back.

Eli gave a respectful "yes, sir" and followed Gladiair into his new cave.

The cave was large and roomy. It had a trough at one end with an ancient looking faucet above it, Eli turned the handle just to make sure water would come even though the trough had already been filled.

Mind unsaddling me now? I'm stiff and sore all over from all this flying. Gladiair complained.

Eli jumped over and unburdened Gladiair quickly, setting his saddle and bags along hooks and shelves towards the back of the room. The large yellow dragon stretched and shook himself all over, much like the dogs did back in the village after getting a bath. He started to lower himself to the ground as if he was going to fall asleep as Eli and Ashwyn looked along the walls for the hose to rinse him off with. Eli spotted it next to the trough, it was a long black hose with a silver spout on the end in the shape of a dragon's head. The water would shoot straight out of the dragon's mouth if only he could figure out how to turn it on.

"Pull the cord next to where you found the hose at" a boy came briskly into the cave, wearing a full riders uniform in dark blue. He was handsome with dark skin, blue eyes, and black hair. He looked to be around the same age as Ashwyn and Eli but neither one recognized him. He walked confidently to a silver cord with a yellow jewel dangling from it and pulled. The water came pouring forth at once as Eli directed the hose at Gladiair. He rolled over onto his back and, let his belly take the full hit. Was that singing? Gladiair was enjoying himself a little too much in his new home.

An indoor bath! I wonder why we don't have one of these in the Caverns back home?

Gladiair continued to roll on the stone floor in every direction as Eli carefully washed every scale as best he could, letting loose sand and twigs littering the floor that swirled until it drained through slits along the walls. Once Gladiair had been thoroughly washed the boy was still standing next to the chain and pulled it a second time which stopped the water.

"Wow, thanks!" Eli enthusiastically replied as he hung the hose back its place, holding out his hand for the boy to shake "I'm Eli, this is Gladiair and that's Ashwyn. We were just bonded yesterday, or well, I guess I was. Ashwyn hasn't found her dragon yet."

"Let me guess" the boys eyes sparkled, and they seemed to dance with joy as he spoke "Amarisk?"

Ashwyn smiled back "How did you know?"

"Oh, trust me, everyone on the Island knows Amarisk. She has been a bit of a handful as we waited for you to arrive. Come on, I'll help you find her, I think I know where she might be" adding as an afterthought "Oh, my name is Farron by the way, and I'm glad you're all here!"

I like him. He has a good spirit Gladiair rumbled.

Ashwyn liked him too. Eli on the other hand wasn't so sure which only made Gladiair burst into laughter, although Ashwyn couldn't see why. Eli stopped at the entrance into Gladiair's room.

"Will you be alright here?" Eli asked. Gladiair had already settled back down in his hay with his eyes closed, purring like a cat.

Yes, I am exhausted. I will probably sleep for the rest of the week. Call if you need me. Gladiair said sleepily.

Ashwyn and Farron were heading out the chamber when Eli caught up.

"Should we check and make sure this is okay with Islan first?" Eli asked.

"Yes, I think someone should check and make sure it is okay with Islan first" came the booming voice of Islan himself from right behind them. The three turned like they had been caught doing something they shouldn't have been to find Islan standing feet broadly spaced and arms crossed over his chest. "I see you have met my son." Ashwyn couldn't believe it! This was Islans son. He had a son?

Eli thought "O great".

"From now on, the two of you are under my direct care. The journey to get here has been more stressful than usual for newly bonded and not bonded yet. Farron, you will help Ashwyn find Amarisk and then get them both settled into their room within the hour. Is that understood?"

Farron was standing stiff and straight "Yes sir!" He replied with a voice as equally intimidating as his fathers.

With a curt bow, he turned and started walking slowing down only when they were all outside of the cavern. "Phew, that was close" he turned and gave Ashwyn a winning smile with eyes still sparkling. He was a little taller than her she noticed as they walked side by side. "Now, let's go find that mischievous dragon of yours".

− 7 −

Ashwyn couldn't figure out why Amarisk, who was supposed to be her dragon, had flown half way to meet her and now that they were finally in the same place, was hiding. Normally she would ponder this sort of thing over with Eli but Farron already proved he knew her, so she ventured to ask "why would she be hiding from me? I don't understand."

Farron laughed, it was a deep hearty laugh that made the hair on her arms stand up. "She isn't really hiding from you. She's mostly hiding from Thunder. He oversees the dragons on the Island, will the young ones at least. She was given a direct order to stay on the Island and wait for your arrival. Once she sensed you were in danger however she left, crossing through the barrier on her own. It was really risky, she could have been killed, she is still young and very much untrained." Farron explained.

Ashwyn felt sorry for Amarisk "will she be punished?"

Farron shook his head no. "Thunder is intimidating and strict, but he is fair. I am sure he will see reason once he hears how she sensed you were in danger. Dragons can't usually sense anything specifically about their humans until they are bonded with them. So, it's pretty amazing she could tell where you were and that you needed help."

Eli was walking behind them but still felt the need to point out, Gladiair had always been able to communicate with both him and Ashwyn from far distances. Farron slowed down so Eli was standing in between him and Ashwyn now "I'm sorry I didn't mean to offend you. The yellow dragon is also very special, I heard he was able to heal you of your blindness. It seems you both have been chosen by two very rare dragons after all" Farron said. Farron seemed genuinely compassionate and kind. Eli was still fuming a bit Ashwyn could tell so took the opportunity to change the subject.

"So, where are we going?" she asked.

They walked down to the main level of the castle once again and were heading out a glass door off to the East. "The gardens. We have beautiful flower gardens here. Amarisk spends most of her free time in them. I think it's because when she was little I would bring her here to play hide and seek with me. I was the youngest on the Island and so was she. We didn't have anyone else to play with." Farron was easy to talk too Ashwyn thought.

The gardens were dark this time of night, lit in occasional spots by small lights sprinkled throughout the flower beds. "Now how do we find an invisible dragon?" Ashwyn pondered out loud more to herself than anyone else.

"Ah ha! Now is where these will come in handy" Farron produced out of his tunic a bunch of freshly washed carrots.

"Carrots?" Ashwyn took them in her hand puzzled as to what she was supposed to do with them.

Farron laughed again "she loves carrots what can I say? Come on."

He took off at a jog to a bench in the middle of the garden surrounded by beautiful yellow rose bushes. The bench was large enough for all three of them to sit on together however Farron and Eli stayed standing. Ashwyn had never felt so tired in her entire life, her eyes were blurring and her whole body was feeling heavy. Not hesitating a moment, she sat down on the bench, holding the carrots out in front of her and waited. Was that bush moving? Do all bushes have sparkling blue eyes? She laughed at herself for being so silly. Out of the darkness strode a small white opalescent dragon with tiny horns fanning out along the fringe covering her neck. Light blue eyes shone brightly as she moved towards Ashwyn without making a sound. She almost looked like a ghost. The dragon was about the size of a draft horse walking carefully up to Ashwyn before sitting down on her hind end and waiting for something. Awkward silence filled the air. Amarisk looked carefully down at the carrots that were now sitting in Ashwyn's lap.

"Oh sorry, would you like one?" Ashwyn asked. Amarisk laughed inside of Ashwyns mind. It sounded like many tinkling bells tapping against each other.

I am glad you are finally here. I have waited years to meet you! And yes, I would like a carrot. Amarisk answered.

"Years? How have you waited years? Did the Queen chose you to bond at so young?" Ashwyn asked as Amarisk polished off the carrots.

Amarisk looked at Farron as if she needed his help to explain.

"Amarisk is still young and a bit shy. She has never been under the orders of the Queen. Amarisk came from here, the Ancient Lands. When humans first came, the White Dragons were Lords of these lands. There were many of them, in fact they are the ones who built the castle you're staying in. Our histories say that the White Dragons allowed us to stay amongst them and learn from them. Then the darkness came trying to destroy all that was good and true, including the White Dragons. They were over powered, it was a great loss to both our races. As a last act of protection, and the greatest act of love possible, the White Dragon Lord sacrificed himself in order to create the protective shield that now covers this Island. The eggs were all that was left of her race." Farron pointed to Amarisk as he continued to speak. "Over the years they have all hatched and gone on to lead great lives. That's been over many hundreds of years. Hers was the last to hatch. She was given into my charge by my dad of course. Ever since she was born she has seen visions of you Ashwyn, and as she's grown older she knew one day that the two of you would bond. It's really unusual. The other dragons who have come to the Island said the Whites were always born special and are considered above royalty amongst other dragons even."

Ashwyn stopped him for a moment "Seen visions of me? Has she always been able to read my mind then, from so far away?"

It sounded unbelievable. Was he blushing? Farron and Amarisk exchanged a glance before Farron put his hand behind his neck and looked down. That can't be good Ashwyn thought.

"Well yes, I mean I think so. We know a lot about you, and your life. I know it seems unfair since you've only just met us, but we feel like we have known you our whole lives" Farron admitted.

Eli wasn't liking the way this was all sounding one bit. "Weren't you supposed to show us to our rooms? We have had a long journey to get here and I for one am ready to get some sleep".

Farron took the hint. "Ah yes, right. Okay then girl, you had best get off to bed as well, and don't worry. Thunder was snoring before I left the caves." He gave Amarisk a wink he strode back through the door that they had come through and back up the sloping walkway. They didn't go clear to the top this time stopping at the second level up and turning down a corridor with a large tapestry hanging from the floor to the ceiling depicting a large white dragon descending out of the sky as if she would land on the very floor they were walking. Stopping at a wooden door with a lily carved on it, Farron opened the door and lit a candle quickly. "Right then, Ashwyn this is your room. You'll find dinner was brought up to you next to the bed, and the washroom is through that door. If you need anything, pull on the cord next to your bed and a servant will be up to help. Okay?" Farron waited for her to confirm she understood all that he had said.

Ashwyn smiled and nodded "thank you Farron. Well I see you tomorrow?" She felt embarrassed almost instantly for asking, as if he had nothing better to do then spend time with her.

He smiled back "I'm afraid I stay pretty busy during the day. My dad has me drilling and studying until almost dark and then I take turns on patrol, but I'll try and find you sometime and see how you're doing. Oh, and tell Amarisk hi for me, I'll be jealous once your bonded, I'll be losing my best friend". He winked closing the door behind him and showing Eli on to his room Ashwyn was certain. Totally spent now that the boys had left she set on the edge of the oversized white fluffy bed with purple pillows and sheets and fell back, still dressed in her traveling clothes, letting sleep over take her.

– 8 –

I think you'll probably want to wake up for this. There is a short white dragon in my cave jabbering about being bonded today. Come and get her or I'm going to have to sit on her to quiet her down. Ashwyn was startled awake by Gladiair's grumpy declaration.

Sitting up in bed she could tell by the way the sun was shining through the room that morning was well underway. Her stomach grumbled reminding her she hadn't eaten anything from the night before. The tray from dinner had been replaced by a tea set next to a puffy purple chair next to the window. Ashwyn decided to freshen up first, heading to the washroom where she found the strangest thing. A box made out of tiles against the wall, held a hose above it similar to the one she had seen used in the dragon rooms last night. She wondered what that was for? Back in her cottage in the mountains, Letti and her had a bathtub in the washroom that they carried buckets of water to when they wanted to freshen up. She concluded that the tile box must be for washing, like the dragons used it, so gave it a try. Amazing! Water rushed over her through the hose. Although it was freezing, it still felt brisk and she was thankful she didn't have to carry any buckets inside for a bath. She couldn't wait to tell Letti about this contraption someday. Drying off, she pulled on her spare green tunic and leggings she had brought. Thankfully someone had the foresight to bring them into the wash room last night. She'd have to try and remember to leave a nice note thanking the servants. Glancing in the mirror she looked much more refreshed. Her long brown hair laid wet against her back which she quickly flipped up into her favorite silver clip left to her by her mother. Her cheeks were rosy and flushed from the shower giving her pale complexion a pleasant glow. One of her most attractive features, her Aunt had told her, was her eyes which were a deep brown with a black ring outlining the iris. Other than that she was fairly short for her age, with a slender build and long, very flat, brown hair. Ashwyn was very grateful for the way she looked though without being arrogant. She looked exactly how she felt a dragon rider should look.

Being thankful for who you are is a wise compliment to give too your Creator. Gladiair again.

I'm coming she tried to appease him for the moment as she found some breakfast. Grabbing fruit and a cold cup of tea off the tray she stood and looked out the window gulping down the food as quickly as she could. The view from her room was breath taking. She could see the white beach directly below her window and then miles and miles of blue ocean stretched out before her. Her room must be on the edge of the Island since no other buildings or road ways were in sight. A knock at the door startled her back to reality as she placed the tea cup back on the tray and carried a piece of bread along with her to answer the door. Eli!

"I thought I had better come and check on you. We've both slept most of the morning away. Gladiair won't stop threatening to eat your new white friend if we don't get up there and remove her from his room immediately" Eli moseyed into the room while eyeing the breakfast platter. Ashwyn gave a laugh as she pushed him back out the room and shut the door behind her.

"You look refreshed" she commented looking him up and down. He was also taller than her by a few inches with brown hair, brown eyes and a pale complexion as well. He was skinny and lean where Farron was muscular.

You're giving that boy an awful lot of thought. I liked him to, but not as much as you apparently. You know it's making Eli jealous. Gladiair scolded.

Ashwyn hoped that was for her ears only and Eli wasn't in on that particular conversation between her and Gladiair.

"It's odd, Amarisk hasn't tried contacting me at all since we arrived on the Island" Ashwyn said in between bites as she finished her bread roll to Eli.

He kept up a brisk pace up the walkway to the dragon caves above. "Gladiair said something last night about she's not supposed to be doing that until you're officially bonded, and not wanting to break anymore rules" Eli explained.

Oh, Ashwyn hadn't considered that. She felt a whole lot better now about the situation. Eli had the same gift as Gladiair, they could both put her worries and fear at ease quickly. Probably because they had all three always been the best of friends and known each other since birth pretty much. She guessed that must be how Farron and Amarisk felt. Although Farron was wearing a dragon riders uniform, so that must mean he also was bonded to his own dragon as well. She'd have to remember and ask him about that the next time she saw him. Before she knew it, they were entering Gladiairs chamber with a very irritated yellow dragon glaring at a bouncy white dragon standing on his tail.

Remove her. He growled at both Eli and Ashwyn causing them both to startle a bit before gaining their senses.

"It seems she has gotten over her shyness" laughed Eli.

Apparently. Although I think she may always be this way around other dragons and is only shy with humans. Gladiair pointed out.

"A wise conclusion" everyone in the room turned at Thunders booming voice. He had actually spoken out loud to all of them! "It would be prideful of me not to speak to all present. I don't particularly like speaking out loud, however I am not above it."

Gladiair did not agree, and for the first time Thunder gave a low chuckle. "Amarisk as for disobeying my orders and leaving the Island. I am disappointed in your lack of obedience and your lack of trust in those who went on the journey before you. I realize that you were worried however for your future rider and thus acted out of love, which is the most courageous act of self-sacrifice another being can make. To that end, at the bonding I will not be giving either of you my blessing or the pendant to leave through the protective shield again until you have both shown yourselves to be obedient. Now, we will continue on to the training dome, where your bonding will be taking place. In order for you to realize what a sacred event this is, I suggest we walk in silence."

Ashwyn wondered if that was for Thunders own sanity. He turned and waited for both dragons to fall in behind him, before starting to walk forward. They continued to follow this procession down through the walkways in the castle and out the main entrance. The sky was a beautiful shade of sapphire with no clouds in sight. The air on the island was fresh and full of moisture, it felt good to Ashwyn to breathe it in awakening all her sense. They walked along a sand pathway covered on both sides by dense flowers and vines, passing occasional statues of deer or large cats in the same white as the castle was made from. If she hadn't been supposed to be walking in silence to contemplate the enormity of the situation she would have liked to ask Thunder what the castle and statues were made of. Eli seemed just as pleased walking along side of her, taking in all the flowers and plants as they strolled to a large building in the shape of a gigantic dome, the training dome. Inside they could hear the clank of sword against sword as Islan fought in the middle of the room with a younger looking man of huge build and brawn. The man had very dark skin, a bald head, deep black eyes and a fierceness Ashwyn would have expected from a powerful dragon. She wondered what his dragon must look like, but she didn't have to wonder long as a sleek black dragon strode into the dome and stood just behind Eli. "Ah, you're here" Islan stopped sparring, bowing to his opponent, as they sheathed their swords. "This will be your combat and arms instructor Titus" gesturing towards the large dark man who was still as a statue looking them over sternly.

He looks fun. Gladiair whispered to Ashwyn and Eli.

"Come forth to the center of the room. Being bonded at the Island is much less of a social event then in the meadows. Amarisk stand in the middle of the sparring ring, Ashwyn kneel before her" they took their positions. "Repeat after me. Where there is injustice we swear to bring justice. Where there is evil we swear to do good. Where this is weakness we swear to be strong. When you need me I will be there. When I need you, I can depend on you. Two lives, becoming one, in this life, and the next. Good. Amarisk, Thunder has been instructing you on how to separate your fires?"

Amarisk held her head high and puffed out her chest, no doubt to look as large and intimidating as she possible could "he has" she also chose to speak out loud.

Islan was pleased as he said "good. Concentrate, draw within yourself and follow Thunders guidance."

Ashwyn probably should have felt terrified, at any moment she knew she would be surrounded by flames. As Amarisk closed her eyes and opened her mouth Ashwyn felt only a great sense of peace and fulfillment, whatever happened, this was her destiny.

White flames surrounded her, blowing back her hair as the flames grew more intense she could see visions of her and Amarisk flying together, happy, joyful, she also saw them in battle and running, surrounded by darkness and falling out of control. Refusing to end the connection the flames continued as she saw the Ancient Islands as they must have been when they began. Large white dragons flew sharing the same opalescent scales of Amarisk. It was mesmerizing watching them constantly change colors subtly as they flew crossing over the Island. The flames died down, Ashwyn and Amarisk faced each other, as if looking at one another for the first time. It was then that Ashwyn noticed a faint glowing yellow rose on the center of Amarisks forehead, had that always been there?

You have one as well. Amarisk spoke back to Ashwyn.

They turned to Islan for explanation, he had gone very pale and stern. However, in that moment all Ashwyn could think of was she couldn't believe she had finally been *chosen by a dragon.*

Amarisk corrected her *more like you were dragon found.*

-9-

The yellow rose was still on Ashwyn's forehead as she stood before the mirror in her room that evening. The rose shimmered like a light dusting of glitter that had fallen in the shape of an open-faced rose. It was small, just above the center of her nose, but still noticeable. She couldn't help but wonder what it could mean. After the bonding, Islan had excused himself saying he had other duties to attend to, and they would speak more of it later. Gladiair and Eli had spent the rest of the afternoon training with Titus while Amarisk and Ashwyn had been measured by the tack master for all the equipment Amarisk would need to carry Ashwyn safely. It was a mundane task that left them both grumpy and tired. Amarisk didn't care for the tack master stretching tape across her girth or from head to tail to try and determine how much extra leather to allow for her growth so a new saddle wouldn't have to be made sooner than necessary. Dragons never quite stopped growing but it slowed down considerably after they reached middle age. Amarisk was still quite young, only a teenager herself and would be expected to grow in random spurts for several years to come. Then after being measured they had to look over different padding, but neither Ashwyn nor Amarisk was sure what sorts of cloth they would prefer. The tack master said some dragons prefer a coarse pad, while others liked soft wool, however they both agreed wool sounded way to hot. Next, they were taken to look over different leather types and colors, at least for once they both knew they wanted something light that would blend into her scales as much as possible. Last was the added adornments they looked at fringes, and jewels, Conchos, and stud fittings. All of it seemed frivolous and unnecessary. Thankfully Amarisk was not a materialistic dragon like some and seemed to enjoy the more modest choice. In the end after many hours of deliberation they settled on a pale colored leather saddle, with small roses and vines stamped up the legs. They still couldn't decide on a pad type, seeing as how they had yet to fly anywhere together, so they left that choice up to the tack master, which seemed to please him also.

When we get the council of others we end up making wise decisions, due to their past experiences. Amarisk said to Ashwyn through their bond.

"That's a wonderful lesson Amarisk, who taught you that?" Ashwyn asked.

All dragons share memories of our ancestors from the past. It is overwhelming to recall all dragon knowledge, so I try to memorize the ones I like best. She simply replied.

She had calmed down considerably since the day they were to be bonded, yet Ashwyn still noticed Amarisk would start to act hyper and a tad immature anytime Gladiair was around. She had a hunch that Gladiair noticed it as well, but he showed restraint and great patience in not correcting her.

"That reminds me!" Ashwyn suddenly remember "we need to ask Islan how to put protective shields around our minds, so others can't read them without our consent."

You mean that YOU need to learn how to put up a protective shield. Dragons are born knowing how to operate our own. Amarisk stated.

"Ah, so true" Ashwyn said knowing that one always felt a tad inferior around a dragon. Feeling exhausted Amarisk had decided to go and spend some time alone in the gardens. Their bond was still new, and it was obvious Amarik still needed some time to herself every once in a while. So Ashwyn had reluctantly gone to her room, hoping to wash up before meeting Eli in the dining hall for dinner. She had heard from a passing dragon rider at the dome that the rest of the riders from her village had arrived on the Islands and they were all to meet for an induction that night. Her stay on the Islands had been so rushed so far and then she was stuck all day with the tack master, she yearned to get out and explore. The landscapes were breathtaking and just behind the castle they were staying in she could make out old fallen down ruins not far off she couldn't wait to go check out. After washing up, and redressing in the new white tunic and purple leggings she was given as her official dragon rider uniform, she took one last glance in the mirror. Perhaps she would need to find some sort of head band or a head wrap to cover her forehead. The yellow rose would probably get her some strange looks and until she understood more about it, she would rather not have to answer awkward questions. Fumbling through her things she found a braided leather headband she tied across the front of her forehead. It was just wide enough to cover the rose, and had the added benefit of making her look like a serious warrior.

Ashwyn heard laughter in her mind *what are you doing?* Amarisks laughter made Ashwyn laugh as well. Okay maybe the warrior part was a bit of a stretch. They hadn't found out what sort of things they would be trained to do yet, and all dragons and riders had certain skills they were best at. In her defense she reminded Amarisk of the other girl rider they had seen this morning practicing in the dome who wore a similar scarf to hold her hair back off her face.

So now we are going to copy the only other girl rider we have found. Amarisk asked.

Feeling sillier by the moment, none the less she stuck true to her decision and left the headband in place....for now. Time to go and find Eli! Leaving her room, she walked down the corridor past the elaborate tapestries of white dragons and went down the sloping stairs to the lower floors. Standing at the base of the stairs looking around the giant room trying to decide which way a dining hall would be when a lady came up to her.

"May I help you miss?" The lady was older with kind sea green eyes and her hair in a neat grey bun atop her head. Ashwyn assumed this must be one of the instructors.

"Yes, thank you, I'm looking for the dining hall please. Are you an instructor here?" Ashwyn asked her.

The kind lady clasped her hands in front of her casually as she spoke "No ma'am. I am a servant here in the castle. This way to the dining hall." What surprised Ashwyn most was her attire. Ashwyn had always pictured servants in long black dresses with pressed white aprons. This lady however wore white silk pants and matching cotton tunic with a gold dragon emblem across the chest. The lady must have noticed Ashwyn's confusion so continued to speak as they walked down a wide hall towards matching wooden doors engraved with giant palm trees.

"We are servants in the sense that we are glad to live here and care for the castle and anyone who stays here. We are free to leave if we ever decided to, yet few do. Prophet Islan takes very good care of us and treats us with kindness. Here we are! Are you ready?" the servant asked.

With a twinkle in her eye the lady waited for Ashwyn to open the large doors. Grasping the pineapple shaped metal handle, Ashwyn felt nervous walking inside. The room was very large, with the same white walls, and large windows that started a few feet above the floor and went many stories up to end in triangles at the top. The views all around were of ancient palm trees, white sands, grassy embankments, tropical wildflowers and the ocean not far off. Row upon row of light colored wooden tables lined up in a cafeteria style. Purple candles shone through tear dropped glass votives on each table. A purple runner ran from where Ashwyn stood, going down the center of the room towards one larger table set up on a platform above the rest. The chairs of that table were intricately carved to look like dragons. Riders were coming out of a side room carrying trays and finding seats. The riders each wore uniforms in the color of their dragon as was the custom. She searched the crowd for Eli who would be wearing the bright yellow shirt he had been given. Her tunic was made from a loser, flowing fabric, his was tighter against his chest matched with bare arms and his pants were black. Walking down the isle to get in line behind the others the smells of exotic spices sifted through the air like incense.

Save some carrots for me if they have any. Amarisk sent a visual of juicy orange carrots which appeared in Ashwyn's mind along with a happy white dragon smacking her lips. Amarisk and her love of carrots.

Islan strode over to Ashwyn "how did the tack fitting go?" He stood casually with his hands behind his back glancing over the room as he waited for her response.

"It was more complicated than we had thought. We decided on a light-colored saddle with roses and vines going up the legs. We had no idea what sort of saddle pad to use so we left that up to the tack master" Ashwyn admitted.

Islan nodded in approval as he continued to survey the room. "Good. How is your room?"

"Beautiful!" she had forgotten to thank him for finding such comfortable accommodations for her. Yet she felt like she must be the only other person on that wing of the castle. She never noticed anyone else coming out of the doors next to hers.

"That's because you are female. There is only one other girl rider here at the time. Her room is next to yours, but she is rarely in it. This reminds me, we need to work on putting up that protection shield in your mind first thing in the morning." Islan said the last words drawn out to emphasize. Ashwyn blushed as he went to take his place at the head of the room. The boy in front of her turned around.

"Islan must like you. I've never seen him talk to the younger riders outside of class before." When she failed to have a response, he continued. "You can call me Skipper. Everyone else does." He was older then Ashwyn, probably in his late teens.

"I'm Ashwyn. Your dragon must be orange? How long have you been training here?" she wondered. The line was moving slowly so it gave them plenty of time to talk.

"Sometimes it feels like I just arrived with all the things to learn but it's really only been four years. I hope we get released soon and assigned a position" he explained.

"Oh, what position do you want?" she asked.

"We are hoping to be navigators. Maps and geography are our favorite subjects. Navigators get to fly between the lands and map out new roads, villages, changes in mountains and so forth. There has been talk though about riders disappearing, so I don't know if they will release us anytime soon" Skipper said.

Ashwyn supposed the rumor had something to do with the greens who were attacked trying to help them to the Islands, but thought it was best not to cause panic. Her turn finally arrived to go down the line. It was hard to choose between all the gorgeous fruits, vegetables, granola, nuts, sweet bread, rolls, and different cuts of meats.

She grabbed as many carrots as she could fit onto her plate next to the sweet bread and fruit she had chosen for herself and went to find a seat. Eli stood out now, towards the back of the room, talking to the girl she had seen in the training dome earlier. The room was nearly full of all the seats being filled and light chatter buzzing in the air.

"Hey! It was harder to find you then I thought" she elbowed Eli lightly as she sat down next to him.

"Really? In this dashing yellow shirt, I didn't stand out?" He was being playful but at the same time seemed a bit disappointed. "This is Raygan" pointing his fork over to the girl next to him. Judging by her black outfit, she also rode a black dragon, the most aggressive of the dragon kind. She looked at Ashwyn and gave a nod but didn't seem very friendly.

"It's nice to meet the only other girl here" Ashwyn ventured.

Raygan continued eating her meat and vegetables. Crystal clanked as everyone turned to see Islan standing at the front of the room waiting for silence.

"Now that all of our new riders have arrived we are ready to begin this year's training. I hope you older riders have enjoyed the past couple of months off. Younger riders, as you get use to the way things are done around here, watch the older riders and seek them for guidance. It also goes without needing to be said I expect all older riders to be helpful to those who are new. We are all a team for the rest of our lives, I expect you all to act like one. The bells will ring tomorrow at first light to begin lessons. In your room tonight, you will find each of your individual schedules have been wrote out for you. Enjoy your meals, afterwards there will be an aerial display on the beach, and then curfew is at ten." Islan concluded his speech.

Ashwyn was giddy with excitement, there was nothing in the world like watching dragons fly. She couldn't begin to imagine what sort of elaborate display they probably performed here on the Islands. Amarisk seemed equally as excited and had already headed down to the beach to get a good spot with Gladiair.

Do you think my rose is the same shade as Gladiair's scales? Amarisk asked Ashwyn.

Ashwyn rolled her eyes at her dragon's musings. As they finished up their meal, placing their empty trays along metal carts that had been rolled out to the edge of each table, they all started walking out in staggered groups towards the beaches. The Island at night was warm, with a soft breeze blowing over them as they strolled down the white sandy paths that curved serpentine like down towards the beach. Torches had been set up along the beach and here or there a large tapestry had been thrown across the sand representing each color of dragon. The riders could stand anywhere they liked, but Ashwyn noticed those of the same color seemed to stay together. She found Amarisk sitting with Gladiair atop of a small knoll a bit away from the rest of the group.

"Didn't want to find the yellow or white tapestry to sit on?" Ashwyn playfully asked knowing her group in general tended to be a bit anti-social.

If we sat on the white, we would be the only ones. Amarisk reminded Ashwyn.

That thought seemed sad, even though she didn't necessarily want to be surrounded by a group of strangers, it felt very isolated to be the only ones. It wasn't that different from her childhood she thought back. Her and Letti had always lived separately from the rest of the village. When she was little, Eli had come to her house by accident. He was supposed to be waiting with his parent's wild mustangs as they traded in the village but had wandered over into their garden when he heard her outside playing. They had become close friends right away and he was the only other child Letti ever let her play with. The crowd started cheering with oooo's and ahhhh's as dragon after dragon flew over the beach like a shooting star. Quick and fierce from one end to the other and then flipping up and separating into pairs representing the different colors present, green, orange, yellow, red, black, blue and purple. The show lasted for hours as Ashwyn watched riders performing acrobatics running on top of their dragons and tossing long shimmering ribbons into the air. Others held mock combats knocking riders into large nets strung along the beach to catch the fallen foe. Gladiair enjoyed those the most and roared loudly as each foe was defeated. Amarisk sat in silence watching each one with cat like concentration. As the show ended and the riders and dragons made their way back to the castle for the evening Ashwyn dropped back to walk alongside Amarisk.

"You were awfully quite tonight, did you like the show?" Ashwyn asked Amarisk.

I did. I come out every year and watch it.

Ashwyn forgot sometimes that Amarisk was born and raised on the Island. "It must have been magical growing up here!"

Amarisks head turned to look down on Ashwyn, peering down at her with cat like blue eyes. *It was……lonely.* Looking back up into the stars.

Can you see the protective shield around the island? Amarisk asked Ashwyn.

Ashwyn stopped walking and looked up at the stars sprinkled across the sky winking back at her. She couldn't see any type of a shield, she tried squinting her eyes, and turning her head to the side a little, but still nothing.

Islan walked up behind her "close your eyes. Now do you feel the part inside of you that feels most like Amarisk? Like when you speak to her, there is a feeling. Do you see it?"

Ashwyn did! It was pure white light, good, and reminded her instantly of all that she knew Amarisk was. Like Amarisk's entire being could be sensed vaguely inside of her, although the depth was bottomless and would take a life times to unravel her being.

"Yes, I found it!" she said excitedly.

Islan continued "Good. Your bond is strong, usually it takes a rider weeks to master that skill in my class. Now, holding onto that feeling, open your eyes and look at the stars again."

Ashwyn opened her eyes and immediately before her eyes she could see a glass like bubble surrounded the Island in a half dome shape. In the excitement of seeing it, she lost her connection with Amarisk and just like that, the bubble was gone. "Why did it disappear again?" Ashwyn wondered.

"Because you stopped thinking of Amarisk, even for a moment, and tried to see it on your own. When you try to do things trusting only in your own abilities, you fail. You must lean on Amarisk, remember your connection and let her live through you, as she will learn to live in you also." Islan admonished.

"That sounds so hard" Ashwyn felt discouraged.

Islan placed his hand on her shoulder forcing her to turn and look at him "if it were easy, we wouldn't call it training. Once you have mastered it, the two of you will live as one no matter what circumstances you find yourselves in. Judging how quickly you picked that lesson up, I have no doubt it won't take long. Now, about that mind of yours. Let's work on putting up a shield."

Walking off the path and pushing through the dense foliage they came to a stone bench amongst pink rose bushes. Islan motioned for Ashwyn to have a seat while he remained standing as Amarisk curled up around the bench, letting her head rest next to Ashwyn's feet. "Now putting up a shield also takes practice. To begin, close your eyes again." He instructed.

"Why does everything involve closing my eyes?" Ashwyn pondered out loud.

"All important battles are fought and won in the mind. The physical we see is much less complex then people make it." Islan instructed. "I want you to focus on all of the thoughts you're having right now, you see them running rampant in your mind going in different directions?"

Ashwyn nodded.

Islan continued, "now isolate your thoughts, bring them under control and quite your mind down." This step took a while, once she felt mostly in control she nodded again. "Now I want you to picture some type of a physical shield that you would see. Some people choose large brick walls, a metal shield clanking in place, a door closing. What did you pick?"

"A door closing" she affirmed.

"Very well, now describe that door to me. It doesn't have to be intricate, just a few details for your mind to focus on. Like what kind of material will your door be? Remember, it needs to be strong, something impenetrable." Islan asked.

"The door is made from marble, it is very heavy, and strong." Ashwyn stated.

Islan continued "now, I'm going to try and enter your mind. You should also be able to feel this now that you are bonded with Amarisk, concentrate."

Ashwyn was starting to perspire from all the focused concentration. She felt a large force running into her, it was so hard and foreign she caught her breath in her throat.

"Good, now I came at you pretty hard, so you would feel it. Remember your enemies will be very subtle. In your free time, practice feeling those around you, the quicker you are at picking up someone pressing into you mentally, the more protected you will be" Islan placed his feet apart. "Next procedure. This time, I am going to come at you more subtly, when you feel me, close your door shut as hard as you can. Ready?"

Ashwyn wasn't sure she would ever be ready.

Don't worry, I am right here with you. He is sneaky, but we can sense him together. I'll help you slam the door, he is in for a surprise! Amarisks words gave Ashwyn new life and determination.

"Ready" Ashwyn said, and then ever so faintly, like the lightest touch of a feather Ashwyn felt Islans presence brush against her mind. SLAM! The door shut fiercely in her mind and when she popped her eyes opened she expected to see Islan flattened on the ground as if the door could have physically knocked him out. In front of her stood a very pleased Islan with a grin wider then she had yet seen showing his perfectly straight, white teeth. Thunder strode up and joined them in the garden during the training session and he also looked pleased.

"Work together like that, and the two of you will be unstoppable. Lessons over for the night. Find your rooms and I'll see you tomorrow first light. Your first lesson, is with me." Islan jumped on top of Thunder and the two rose powerfully into the air and off into the night. Ashwyn fell asleep that night feeling whole, like she was no longer on her own, and could face anything with Amarisk. The purring she heard in her mind from her beautiful white dragon, told her that Amarisk felt exactly the same way. Light suddenly poured across her face as Farron burst into the room....

Author's Note

If you're reading this, then I want to thank you for sticking with me through this amazing story! I hope you found it to be inspiring, fun and entertaining.

More of Ashwyn's adventures are yet to come! Until we meet again, may you all chase after your dreams in life and become all you were created to be!

I always enjoy hearing from fellow readers you can send me a message through face book at https://www.facebook.com/DragonFound/

Also please consider leaving a review on Amazon. Thank you!

Made in the USA
Middletown, DE
04 January 2019